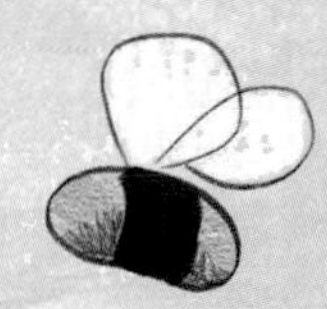

PEEK-A-BOO
BUNNY

For the gorgeous Ava-Lucia:
hop little bunny, hop hop hop! xxx

Also by Holly Surplice:
ABOUT A BEAR

First published in paperback by HarperCollins Children's Books in 2013

1 3 5 7 9 10 8 6 4 2

ISBN: 978-0-00-741437-6

HarperCollins Children's Books is a division of HarperCollins Publishers Ltd.

A CIP catalogue record for this title is available from the British Library.

Visit our website at: www.harpercollins.co.uk

Printed in China

PEEK-A-BOO BUNNY

Holly Surplice

HarperCollins *Children's Books*

Bunny's with his
friends today,

and there's one game they
LOVE to play!

Bunny,
Bunny,
don’t you peek…

Bunny, Bunny, hide and seek!

9
10

Bunny
jumping on
the spot,

Bunny coming, ready or not!

Bunny, Bunny,
running fast,
rushes by
and speeds
right past.

Bunny hopping here
and there…

Bunny, Bunny,
misses Hare.

Bunny, Bunny,
sniffs around,

but does not like
the smell he's found!

Bunny trying
not to fall,

misses friends
both big
and small.

Bunny busy stretching high,
fails to see what Mole can spy.

Bunny searching on the ground,

if only he would
turn around!

Bunny, Bunny,
looking down,

his smile
is turning
to a frown.

Bunny,
Bunny, what
to do?

Bunny, Bunny…

PEEK
-A-
BOO!